TERRY DEARY

Victorian Tales

The Sea Monsters

Inside illustrations by
Helen Flook

BLOOMSBURY EDUCATION
AN IMPRINT OF BLOOMSBURY

LONDON OXFORD NEW YORK NEW DELHI SYDNEY

Victorian Tales

The Sea Monsters

This second edition first published 2016 by
Bloomsbury Education, an imprint of Bloomsbury Publishing Plc
50 Bedford Square, London, WC1B 3DP

www.bloomsbury.com

First published in 2012 by A & C Black Limited.

Bloomsbury is a registered trademark of Bloomsbury Publishing Plc

A CIP catalogue for this book is available from the British Library

ISBN: 978 1 4729 3983 8 (paperback)

Printed and Bound by CPI Group (UK) Ltd, Croydon CR0 4YY

1 3 5 7 9 10 8 6 4 2

Chapter 1

Canvey Island, near London, 31 March 1838

Ben Leary picked up the pen, dipped it in the ink-pot and smiled. He began to write.

Dear Cousin Grace

It is amazing that we are both sailing to the United States at the same time but on different ships.

I have a job in the boiler room of the Great Western steamship. It is the greatest steamship the world has ever seen. Of course

Suddenly he threw down the pen and spattered black spots over the desk. He walked to the door. He opened it. He looked at the sky. He shook his fists and cried, "I can't say that – I can't, I can't, I can't."

Seagulls squawked back at him. "Kee-ark, kee-ark, kee-ark." The mighty paddle-wheels at each side of the ship

churned and frothed and chopped and slapped at the sea.

Ben squinted up at the gulls through his thick brown fringe of hair. "Did you say 'You can'?" he asked.

"Kee-ark."

"Then I will say it." The boy stepped back into the cabin and picked up his pen again. He wrote:

Of course Mr Brunel built Great Western and it is much bigger and faster than your ship, Sirius. We will get to New York first. But don't worry, I will wait on the docks for you.

Ben shook his fists again. "Oooh, that is such a cruel tease," he giggled. "But I don't care. Grace thinks she's the queen of

Ireland. Grace gives herself airs and graces … hah! Grace full of graces," he cried, and laughed till his sides hurt.

There was a lot of noise on the deck of *Great Western* and Ben stepped out to have a look. A man stood on the afterdeck and the crew of the ship were walking towards him.

The man's side-whiskers were thick and curling. A fat cigar was clamped into his mouth and a top hat perched on his large, wise head. It was the great engineer Isambard Kingdom Brunel himself. Sparks flew from the cigar as the sea breeze blew.

"My friends, this trial is a success. We will arrive in Bristol tomorrow, pick up our passengers and set off across the Atlantic Ocean to New York. We will make history. The first steamship to cross the Atlantic."

"What about *Sirius*?" a coal-blacked boilerman called.

Brunel pushed his top hat to the back of his head. "*Sirius* is too small. She can't carry enough coal to get her across the Atlantic. She will have to use her sails, you'll see ... and a sailing ship can't win a steamship race. In fact, sailing ships won't win anything any more. From now on, sailing ships are dead."

"Three cheers for Mister Brunel," a ship's officer cried and raised his cap in the air. "Hip, hip ..."

"Fire!" came a cry from behind Ben.

Everybody turned to see a sooty stoker choke on smoke as he climbed up the stairs from the boiler room. "There's a fire below decks," he gasped. "Oil rags caught alight."

"Calm, gentlemen, calm," Brunel shouted. "You all know what to do."

Seamen hurried to pick up pumps and suck the water from the sea. Ben helped to carry one of the hoses through the door and into the hot smoke coming from below.

Water gushed down and hissed and spat and spluttered as it hit the orange glow below. The water turned to steam but the crackle of burning wood stopped.

Isambard Brunel stood at the top of the stairway and looked down into the darkness.

"Sorry, sir," the boilerman coughed and sobbed. "A shovel of hot ashes fell on the floor and set light to a pile of oil rags."

Brunel nodded. "But the steam engine hasn't been harmed?" he asked.

"I don't think so, sir."

"I'll have a look. Someone pass me a lantern," the great engineer said. He placed his foot on the top step and began to walk down.

"Careful, sir, those steps will be wet and slippery and ..."

Brunel gave a cry and tumbled down into the dark. There were bumps, clumps and crashes. Then a terrible silence.

"Oh, dear," Ben moaned.

"Kee-ark," a seagull laughed.

Chapter 2

Cork, South Ireland, 4 April 1838

Patrick Leary stood on the deck of the steamship *Sirius* and looked across the endless Atlantic Ocean. "I can't see America," he said.

His sister, Grace, had the same dark hair but she was a year older and a little taller. "Climb up the mast, why don't you, and maybe you can see it from there."

"Really?" the boy cried.

"No, *not* really," she groaned, and slapped him on the shoulder. "Sometimes,

Patrick, I think you haven't the brains you were born with. America is three hundred miles away ... or do I mean three thousand? Anyway it's the longest way. You can't see three thousand miles. No one can."

Patrick pulled a face. "I saw the moon last night and that's a million miles."

Grace raised her hand to slap him again but the boy ducked and ran along the deck, pushing past passengers and tripping over their luggage. He picked himself up, turned and put out his tongue.

The girl glared.

"Patrick, will you remember you're not a child any more. You are a cabin boy on the greatest ship that ever sailed from Ireland. You have to serve our important passengers. And when we get to America, they won't let you stay if you behave like that. You know what Uncle James said?"

"He said they'd make me a slave and send me out to pick cotton," the boy muttered.

"And it'll serve you right, so it will," she said. "Cousin Ben wrote to say he'll be waiting for us and he won't put up with you. He'll send you back to Ireland."

Patrick hung his head and murmured, "Sorry, sis."

"Now get yourself along to Captain Derry and start your cabin-boy work. When we set sail, and finish work for the night, I'll see you in the crew quarters for supper. I'm off to give the cabins a final polish before we set off. Go on with you."

The deck of the ship was crowded with passengers and sailors. Men with sacks ran up the gangplank, loading coal till the ship was full and low in the water.

Patrick was sent up and down the stairs to the cabins below decks, carrying cases and serving the rich folk with food and wine. His new starched collar rubbed at his neck and he sweated in his smart black suit.

When he climbed back on deck for the tenth time the smoke from the funnel filled the air with fumes that made his eyes water.

The passengers were all on the deck and waving to the hundreds of friends and people of Cork City who lined the dockside.

The whistle on the funnel screamed and the people fell silent.

Captain Derry stood on the top deck and held up a hand. His face was handsome but worn as boot leather and his voice as harsh as the steam whistle.

"Welcome aboard *Sirius*," he shouted. "We are about to set off to New York on the tide. But first I wanted to give you some amazing news. As you know a ship has never crossed the Atlantic Ocean before under steam power only, without the help of sails. We wanted to be the first."

Someone in the crowd gave a cheer and the people on the decks and the dock clapped loudly.

"Over in England," the captain went on – and the word 'England' was met with boos – "Over in England, there is a clever man called Isambard Kingdom Brunel. And he has built a bigger ship than our *Sirius*."

The crowd groaned.

"We're beaten before we start," someone sighed.

"But," Captain Derry cried over the moans, "the mighty Isambard Brunel has had an accident. Well, to be honest it's a

couple of accidents. First his ship caught fire ..." Captain Derry gloated.

"That can't happen here, can it?" a pale-faced woman with an owl-screech voice screamed.

"No, no, no, sure it can't," the captain said quickly to calm the fear that ran across the deck like a cold Atlantic wave. "We have the best stokers in the world

aboard. But Mr Big-Brain Brunel fell and hurt himself. He won't be sailing with his *Great Western*."

There were a few heartless cheers to greet the news of the engineer's injuries.

"But it also means they won't set off on time. My friends in England tell me they'll be four days behind. This is *not* a race, of course ..."

"No, no, no, it's not," the passengers nodded.

"Yes, it is," Grace whispered to Patrick. "I'd love to be on the New York docks to greet cousin Ben. Smug cousin Ben, writing letters like that to gloat about getting there first."

"This is not a race, as I say," Captain Derry went on. "But we're going to win it anyway," he finished with a wide grin on his handsome face.

"So what are we waiting for?" the pale and shrieking woman cried, excited.

"Erm ... the tide, madam. The tide."

Chapter 3

Avonmouth, Bristol, 8 April 1838

Ben stood on deck and looked across to the city of Bristol. The April sun was bright and fresh but the feeling of gloom was as great as *Great Western*'s steam-hot, oil-scented, cog-clattering engine-room deep below the decks.

"Seven," Captain Wright sighed. "We were supposed to have over fifty passengers on this voyage. They heard about the fire. They lost their nerve. How many are left?"

"Seven," Ben said as he held the captain's mug of tea.

"Seven," the captain sighed. "Not much work for a cabin boy to do with just seven passengers."

"No, sir."

"So you can stay in England if you like."

Ben's mouth opened and closed silently like a horrified herring.

"N-no, sir. I want to be in New York to meet my Irish cousins. I wrote and told them I'd see them there."

The captain spread his hands. "And you shall."

Ben screwed up his face to stop the tears. "I told them I'd be there first. I said I'd be waiting on the dock to greet them."

Suddenly Captain Wright looked up. His gloom seemed to lift.

"And so you shall, Ben lad. Yes, of course. We may have lost our passengers but we haven't lost the race."

Ben shook his head. "The *Sirius* has four days' start. Can we catch her?"

The captain's brown eyes glowed.

"Catch her and beat her. You heard what Mr Brunel said. *Sirius* is too small to carry the coal she needs to sail the Atlantic. She'll have to keep her fires

low and her paddles crawling round.
Thanks for reminding me, my lad, you've
made this voyage into something like
sport."

"A race?"

"A race," the captain nodded. He turned
to an officer and called, "Cast off the ropes,
Mr Anderson."

"The tide isn't full yet," the sailor warned
him.

"No, but I want to be ready to leave as soon as it is. We're in a race, man. If this was a horse track the starter would have his flag in the air and the horses lined up. Cast off."

The order ran through the ship like steam through a boiler pipe. The midnight faces of the crew turned noon-bright with excitement.

Tugboats hauled the world's largest ship into the middle of the River Avon. Coal was shovelled into the fiery furnaces till sweat on the stokers washed the coal dust from their faces.

When the tugs reached the frothy, choppy waters of the Atlantic, they cast their ropes off. Captain Wright shouted the order and the engines began to turn paddle wheels that were as high as a house.

England began to shrink and vanish and the empty, roaring miles of waves lay ahead. When evening came and dinner was served, one lady passenger demanded that Captain Wright entertain them. "We can't play cards for two weeks," the woman sniffed.

Ben had been serving the captain some roast beef and whispered in his ear, "The family used to recite poetry after dinner, sir. I know that poem about the French sailor who stayed on his sinking ship. 'Casabianca'."

Captain Wright snapped, "For goodness sake, Ben. I'm sure the ladies and gentlemen want to hear about a ship that catches fire and explodes."

"'Casabianca'?" the lady cried. "Oh, I love that poem," she said and clapped her hands. "Listen everyone, our cabin boy is going to tell us the tale of 'Casabianca'."

Captain Wright shrugged and Ben began.

"The boy stood on the burning deck
Where all but he had fled;
The flame that lit the battle's wreck
Shone round him o'er the dead."

That evening Ben made a week's wages in the money the passengers threw into his cap. And every evening he found a new poem to recite or song to sing ... songs he had learned from his Irish cousins, Patrick and Grace.

And every hour *Great Western* sped across the dark Atlantic and brought the cousins closer.

Chapter 4

Sirius, The Atlantic Ocean, 21 April 1838

Sirius ploughed through the waves like a walrus through treacle. The decks pitched and swayed as the uncaring, clumsy waves lifted her and dropped her.

Patrick was the smallest boy on board, so he was given the job of climbing to the top of the mast as the look-out.

"Can you see *Great Western*?" Captain Derry asked.

The wind and the rolling ship whipped the mast till the boy was giddy and sick.

He forced himself to look back over the stern of the ship. Back to where Ireland lay three thousand miles away.

There was nothing but an empty grey sea. No wisp of smoke to show a steamship following. Every day he looked for smoke as if *Sirius* was being chased by a fire-breathing dragon.

"No, sir," Patrick called.

"Turn around, Patrick lad."

The boy clung to the ropes and his frozen hands almost let go as he struggled to turn towards the bow of the ship. The smoke from the funnel was pigeon blue but the flecks of soot were black, and stung him when one landed in his eye.

"Can you see the coast of America?"

The view ahead was a little blurred. Not a hard line like the view over the stern.

Maybe that was land about fifty miles away ... maybe.

"I'm not sure, sir," Patrick shouted.

"Come down lad," Captain Derry said and gave a sigh. He turned to Grace. "My maps show we should be fifty miles from New York."

"That's good," Grace said.

She smiled as Patrick's iced hands let go of the rough rope and he dropped the last few feet and into his sister's waiting arms. She set him down gently on the swaying deck.

"That's bad," the captain said.

Grace had worked in a shop back in Cork and she knew how to do her sums. "At this speed we'll be there by morning," she said.

"That's the problem ... we can't keep up this speed. The coal bunker is empty now.

We're running on coal dust, and getting so little heat we'll just get slower and slower."

"So we'll lose the race?" Patrick groaned.

"We will," the captain said.

The boy looked at his sister.

"Can you see it, Grace? Cousin Ben standing on the dock side at New York waiting for us. And I bet, I bet, I bet he has a big fat grin on his big fat face. I hate him."

Grace wrapped an arm around his shoulder. "You don't mean that, Patrick. Ben is always kind when we meet him."

"Yes, but he always has to *win* when we play games. We had a poetry reading last year and he even made that into a contest. *And* he had to win."

Grace nodded. "He was very good. He recited that poem, 'The boy stood on the burning deck,' and it made me cry."

"Soppy poem. I like the one the Irish boys in Cork harbour used to sing..." Patrick threw back his head, and his voice was clear as the wind whistling through reeds.

"*The boy stood on the burning deck,*
The flames 'round him did roar;

He found a bar of Ivory Soap
And washed himself ashore."

The weary crew and passengers laughed and the sound of their clapping could be heard over the slapping of the paddles in the sea.

Suddenly one voice was raised louder than any.

"*The boy stood on the burning deck –* that's it, Patrick," Grace cried. "That's what we need to win the race."

"A boy?" the captain asked.

"No, a burning deck! Listen ... here's what we'll do," Grace said and the curious crew gathered around her.

Chapter 5

Great Western, The Atlantic Ocean,

22 April 1838

Ben was weary from performing every night for the passengers. Each tiresome day was spent learning a new poem from the captain's fat book of poetry.

The passengers loved to hear the poems but they liked the *long* ones best. And they didn't want them read from the book. They wanted Ben to recite from memory and do actions with them, as if he were Mr Punch in a puppet show.

Above all, they liked the miserable poems. The tales of death and disaster, heroes and horrors, warriors and wonders.

Tonight it would be "The *Revenge*", the story of a gallant little warship called the *Revenge*.

The captain and the seven passengers sat around the large captain's table eating chicken stewed in red wine. They didn't look very happy.

"Do you want me to do my poem?" Ben asked when the plates had been cleared and the rich folk were sitting with coffee to drink and chocolates to munch.

"I suppose so," Captain Wright said with a sigh. "We need cheering up. We are just a day away from New York and *Sirius* should be in sight if we are going to win the race. She should have run out of coal by now. Mr Brunel said she would."

The seven passengers all sighed. The sound was like a winter wind in a Christmas chimney.

Ben set off with the terrific tale of the little British ship that met with a fleet of huge Spanish galleons. The *Revenge*'s captain could have run away but he chose to stay and fight. The ship was smashed by the Spanish cannon but still he wouldn't give in...

"For he said, 'Fight on! fight on!'
Tho' his vessel was all but a wreck."

The Spanish were shattered but the damage to *Revenge* was too great. The next storm sank her.

Ben finished with a heartbreaking sob on the last lines ...

"And the little Revenge herself went down
by the island crags
To be lost evermore in the main."

Ben smiled and bowed. The captain looked stormier than any storm cloud.

"Stupid lad," he snarled.

"I thought you liked songs of the sea ..." Ben began.

"We are a mighty ship like a galleon – we are trying to defeat a poor little, useless piece of Irish matchwood called *Sirius*. We do *not* want to hear about a brave little winner. We need a poem about a brave and battling big ship, you donkey. Get below decks and scrub the boilers before I throw you overboard to swim with the fishes!" Captain Wright roared.

"Eeeek!" Ben squeaked before he turned and ran.

* * *

Next morning he climbed on deck at first light when he heard the cry.

"Smoke ahead ... it must be *Sirius*. She's twenty miles ahead of us – but it looks like she's almost reached New York."

The crew groaned.

"Lost evermore," Ben moaned and shook his fist at a circling seagull.

"Awk," the seagull replied.

"How did *Sirius* do that?" the captain cried.

Chapter 6

New York, 23 April 1838

Grace laughed when she met Ben on the docks of New York.

"Ah, Ben, it's so good to see you," she said.

"What kept you?" Patrick asked cheekily.

Ben glared at him. "You had four days' start," he said.

"Sure, but you said you would be here first," Grace replied and her eyes sparkled in the spring sunshine.

She took out his letter and wafted it in

front of his nose. "Look, cousin, it says here ..."

"Master Brunel said your little Irish ship had no chance," Ben argued, stubborn. "You should have run out of coal."

"And we did, clever Ben," Patrick said.

Ben looked at him sharply. "So you

used your sails? You didn't cross the ocean by steam alone? You lost the race?"

Grace shook her head. "We ran out of coal – but there's more than coal will make a fire to heat the boiler. I remembered that when young Patrick recited the poem about the boy who stood on the burning deck. It gave me the idea," she said.

"If we had no coal, we could burn the deck," her brother nodded. "Burning deck, see?"

"Well, maybe not the *deck* exactly. But anything on the ship made of wood," Grace said.

They began to walk into the busy city, dodging the horses and wagons that clattered through the crowded streets.

"First, we burned the furniture," Patrick explained. "Chairs and tables and

cupboards, you know?"

"Yes. I know what furniture is," Ben said sourly.

"We sighted New York twenty miles away just as we sighted you twenty miles behind," Grace said. "But we'd burned every last bunk bed and table."

"So the ship's carpenter climbed up the mast and cut off the top," Patrick went on. "We chopped it up for firewood. It burned well, so we cut off some more. Soon we had no mast left and New York was just a mile away. A few of the planks from the deck were thrown in the boiler and we just made it."

Ben shook his head. "That's cheating,"

he muttered.

Grace wrapped an arm around his

shoulders. "Come on, Ben, you lost the race. But everybody knows your *Great Western* is the greatest ship on the oceans. She's the fastest ship ever to sail the Atlantic and you were there on board when she did it. You should be proud."

The boy nodded. "I suppose so."

"And we all got here safe," Patrick added.

"We had the luck of the Irish."

"So come along to the lodging we found for us," Grace said, leading the way through the tall wooden buildings that shaded the sun. "The landlady will have a fine dinner ready for us."

"My first American dinner," Ben said, cheering up. "What will it be?"

Grace stopped and frowned. "Irish stew, of course. What else?"

True History

The *Sirius* only made one more trip across the Atlantic and then went back to paddling from London to Cork. Nine years after her great Atlantic adventure she was caught in a storm off the coast of Ireland and sank. 20 people were drowned. She wasn't a great or even a lucky ship, but she will always be the first steamship to cross the Atlantic.

The story of an Atlantic ship crew burning the ship to finish the journey became a famous one. A writer called Jules Verne used that true tale as part of his famous adventure story, 'Around the World in Eighty Days'.

The *Great Western*'s journey to America took fifteen days and over the next eight years made 60 crossings.

Isambard Brunel went on to build even greater ships to cross the Atlantic.

Brunel became ill in 1859, just before the *Great Eastern* made her first voyage to New York. He died ten days later at the age of 53.

The poem 'Casabianca' ('The boy stood on the burning deck') is a poem written by British poet

Dorothea Hemans, in 1826. It became one of the most popular poems in Victorian Britain. Thousands of children learned it at school and recited it at parties.

You try

1. A lot of people made fun of 'Casabianca' – they changed the words the way Patrick did in the story. Can YOU write a new verse? Start with:
'The boy stood on the burning deck...'

Remember, when you write the second line it will have to rhyme with the fourth line. So make sure the last word is easy to rhyme. Don't write...

'The boy stood on the burning deck,

The flames were red and orange...'

... or you'll make it very difficult!

2. Imagine you had a steam ship like *Sirius* which could cross the Atlantic. If it stops to take on more wood and coal it could go around the world.

Name FIVE places YOU would visit in the world. Why did you choose them? What do you think you might see there? Who might you meet?

3. There are now sailing competitions where prize money is given for the winner. In 2016 the Sailing World Cup Final was held in Melbourne, Australia, and the prize was over £100,000. Write down FIVE things you would buy if you won that £100,000.

Tudor Tales

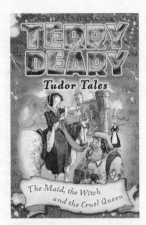

Exciting, funny stories based on real events...
welcome to the Tudor times!

Terry Deary's Shakespeare Tales

If you liked this book
why not look out for the rest of
Terry Deary's Shakespeare Tales?
Meet Shakespeare and his
theatre company!

World War II Tales

 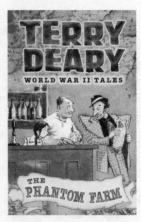

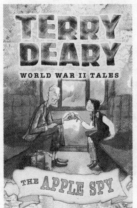 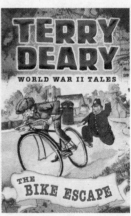

Exciting, funny stories based on real events...
welcome to World War II!